Praise for other Arthurian novels by
Kim Iverson Headlee

*Dawnflight*
"Intense."
~ *USA Today*

*Morning's Journey*
"I love the way Headlee infuses historic languange
to really flesh out the cultures and history of her world.
Overall strong characters, good pacing and a vibrant world
make [*Morning's Journey*] a compelling read."
~ *CS Fantasy Reviews*

*King Arthur's Sister in Washington's Court*
"Solidly entertaining."
~*Publishers Weekly*

# Twins

*Kim Iverson Headlee
Stories make us greater.*

# Kim Iverson Headlee

### Pendragon Cove Press

*Published by*
*Pendragon Cove Press*

*Twins*
Copyright ©2017 by Kim Headlee

All rights reserved, including the right to reproduce this book or portions thereof in any form, with the exception of brief excerpts for the purpose of review.

This book is a work of fiction. Names, characters, places, and incidents are products of the authors' imaginations or are used fictitiously. Any resemblance to actual events or locales or persons, living or dead, is entirely coincidental.

ISBN-13: 978-1-19737487-6-2
ISBN-10: 1-97374876-2
E-book ISBN: 0-9971202-8-2

Cover art copyright ©2015 by Natasha Brown
Photo credits:
"Redhead warrior" (Gwenhwyfach)
© by Syda Productions, Dreamstime ID 5329518
Clothing for Gwenhwyfach
© by fxquadro, Depositphotos ID 68915815
"Redhead woman" (Gwenhwyfar)
© by Eevlva, Dreamstime ID 45719028

Interior art ©2015 by Kim Headlee
Pendragon Cove Press logos copyright ©2014 by Natasha Brown

# Twins

A Dragon's Dove Chronicles Novella

and the genesis of
Book 6, *Sundown of a Dream*

## Chapter 1
### The Idea

GYANHUMARA nic Hymar, Chieftainess of Clan Argyll of Caledonia and High Queen of Brydein, was dead.

Arthur descended the mausoleum's steps to await Gyan's casket. *Even the storm clouds have come to pay tribute*, thought their youngest daughter, Gwenhwyfach ferch Arthur, as she drew her cloak closed against the chilling October drizzle.

She glanced at her twin sister, Yfarryn, standing opposite her at the mausoleum's entrance. After the ornate oaken casket passed between them, borne on one side by Gawain, Gareth, and Medraut and on the other by Bedwyr, Uwain, and Angusel, she noticed her sister's chin was trembling. Of course Yfarryn would be feeling their mother's loss more, Gwenhwyfach realized with a surge of envy. As firstborn daughter, Yfarryn bore the Brytoni version of their mother's given name—Gwenhwyfar, "white shadow"—and had spent far more time in her company, being trained to assume duties within Clan

Argyll that would fall to Gwenhwyfach only if Yfarryn were to die childless.

With such an exalted role to fill, Yfarryn in her humility had for years preferred to be known as the raw bar of iron used by a farrier to fashion horseshoes.

Gwenhwyfach had never appreciated that choice as much as she did today, now that their mother had become a white shadow herself.

Lannchu mac Eileann of Clan Alban of Caledonia shifted closer to Yfarryn and slipped his arm behind her back. The look she turned upon him was suffused with gratitude and love. Gwenhwyfach suppressed a snort. Yfarryn wouldn't remain childless for long if she had her way. Her legendary infatuation with Chieftain Angusel's son had sparked more than one disagreement between Arthur and Gyan.

A chanting Abbot Dafydd and two censer-swinging acolytes followed the casket and its bearers into the mausoleum. The prayers competed with the thud of apples in the surrounding orchard being ripped from their branches by the raging wind. One sound, however, emerged with terrible finality: the scrape of stone against stone as the sarcophagus's lid was pushed into place. It felt to Gwenhwyfach as though someone were raking a dagger across her heart.

The abbot and his acolytes emerged from the tomb, followed by Uwain, Bedwyr, and Gwenhwyfach's half cousins, Gawain, Gareth, and their youngest brother, Medraut. Gwenhwyfach offered Medraut a tentative smile.

Had anyone asked her why her heart fluttered and her breath shortened whenever Medraut was near, she would have been hard pressed to form a coherent answer. Myriad details attracted her: his handsome face, charming smile, battle-hardened body, swift wit, wise counsel—not unique attributes, certainly. Why other men failed to turn Gwenhwyfach's head when Medraut always did, she couldn't begin to fathom.

He didn't see Gwenhwyfach's smile because he had directed his attention upon her sister. Yfarryn and Lannchu stiffened and stepped apart.

Gwenhwyfach watched Medraut join his brothers, feeling a stab of yearning for what would never be.

If the others had appeared sorrowful, Angusel was the picture of grief. He had been the first to find Gyan in Port Dhoo-Glass's serpent pit and would forever bear the anguish that he had failed to save her life. He passed a hand over his face and sank to his knees, head bowed, at the top of the stairs. "Lady Gwenhwyfar, Lady Gwenhwyfach, I am so—very—sorry..." His voice caught and tears sprang to his eyes.

Lannchu bent to coax him to stand. "Father, we know you did your best. There is no shame in that."

Angusel shrugged off his son's hand and got to his feet unassisted. "My best wasn't good enough. That is the greatest shame, lad." He gazed at Gyan's daughters. "My ladies, can you forgive me?"

Yfarryn gasped, hand to mouth, and fled into the mausoleum. Echoes of her sobs drifted up, punctuated by Arthur's muted tones.

Gwenhwyfach reached for Angusel's battle-ravaged hands. He hadn't earned the title of na Lann-Seolta, bestowed by the High Queen, for naught. But all the blade-cunning in the world never could have vanquished the poison that had stolen her life. "Chieftain Angusel, your son is right. Please do not blame yourself." She hoped the strength of her grip conveyed the sincerity of her feelings. "I do not."

He squeezed her hands and released them. "You are most gracious, Lady Gwenhwyfach, and I thank you." She didn't believe he had forgiven himself, but she hoped this was a start. He bowed and withdrew to stand beside Lannchu.

Yfarryn's sobs had quieted, and Gwenhwyfach deemed it time to pay her respects. She laid back her hood, drew a deep breath, and descended the steps.

Pungent incense permeated the narrow chamber. Wan light from four tall tapers battled the gloom. Arthur stood at the head of the sarcophagus, flanked by Yfarryn, his hand caressing the contours of the effigy's face. He glanced up at Gwenhwyfach's approach and his hand stilled to rest against one gray cheek. "It's so hard to believe..."

"I know, Father," Gwenhwyfach said, drawing her sword. She held the naked blade, hilt up, before her face. She had chosen the warrior's path, hoping it would forge a stronger bond between her and her mother, to make up for the years they'd been apart. But now... "I know."

She sheathed the sword and neared the sarcophagus, reaching for the effigy's closest hand, which curled around the stone sword's hilt. The granite felt warm beneath her fingertips, creating the illusion that her mother wasn't dead, that somehow her life force, which had burned so vibrantly mere days before, had not been extinguished.

Gwenhwyfach shook her head to clear it of such fanciful nonsense. The High Queen was dead. Nothing could change that.

Yfarryn didn't want to leave the tomb. Leaving meant having to begin a life without her mother's guidance; a joyless life once her father made the expected proclamation.

Blinking back tears, she regarded her sister. Fach—a nickname Gwenhwyfach detested because it meant "small," so Yfarryn saved its spoken use for when she was angriest at her—looked ever so calm and assured in her silver and boiled leather ceremonial armor. Yfarryn resented Fach for being able to pay tribute in a manner their mother would have appreciated more so than anything Yfarryn might do.

*Not true*, Yfarryn reminded herself. Fighting the tremors in her voice, she sang the Caledonian warrior's lament. Having to substitute her mother's name into the lyrics wrenched her heart, and it was all she could do to keep the song from dissolving into sobs. But it was comforting too, and for that she was grateful.

When the last notes had echoed into silence, she sank to her knees beside the sarcophagus as if the music had been the only thing supporting her. She pressed her cheek and palm to the granite panel, willing herself to wake from this hideous dream.

Her father stooped to whisper, "Beautifully done, Yfarryn. Thank you. Gyan—I'm sure she would have loved it." Yfarryn looked up to see him drag the back of a hand across his eyes. He stood and offered her his hand. "Come. We must go."

Yfarryn placed her hand in his, stood, adjusted her cloak and skirts, and ascended with her father and sister into the bleak wilderness of her future.

AWAITING THEM near the mausoleum, surrounded by a detachment led by a very irritated-looking Cai, was a delegation of toga-garbed men Gwenhwyfach didn't recognize.

Cai stepped forward and saluted Arthur. "Forgive me, Your Majesty, but these men"—on Cai's lips, the word sounded like an epithet—"refused to be put off. They claim to be ambassadors on an urgent mission from Rome."

The delegation's leader eyed Cai with disdain before bowing toward Arthur. Gwenhwyfach dropped her hand to her sword hilt. The gesture did not go unnoticed by the visitors. The delegate said, "Please accept our sincerest condolences and apologies, Your Majesty. We would not have intruded upon so sorrowful an occasion were our mission not of the utmost importance."

"What can be so bloody important—" At a flick of Arthur's hand, Cai fell silent. He crossed his arms, glaring.

Arthur prompted the man to continue.

He cleared his throat, squared his shoulders, and jutted his jaw. His companions adopted similar poses. "It has come to the attention of Emperor Lucius that the province of Britannia—"

"Province!" roared Cai. Arthur stared at him.

"The province of Britannia," continued the ambassador, "is a number of years delinquent in sending tribute to Rome." Gwenhwyfach glanced at Cai, whose coloring indicated he was headed for an apoplectic fit. Her father looked none too happy either. Heeding neither man, the delegate consulted a scroll he had been carrying in a leather tube. "One hundred twenty-seven years, to be exact. Emperor Lucius has commissioned us to negotiate terms for the settlement of this debt, as well as future arrangements."

While Cai and others exploded into either rage or laughter, Angusel pitched his voice to address Arthur over the din. "It is obvious to me, Your Majesty, that this barbarian upstart who has the audacity to call himself the Emperor of Rome has heard of the greatness of Brydein and has decided to see what he can loot from us, now that Rome has been picked clean." The ambassadors began sputtering protests, but Angusel stalked toward them, expression fierce and sword half-drawn. "Give the word, Arthur, and this matter ends here."

Arthur's face was as stony as the tomb at his back, and just as unyielding. "Chieftain Angusel, this is neither the time nor the place to render such a decision." He regarded Bedwyr and Cai. "Take your detachment and introduce our esteemed ambassadors to Port Dhoo-Glass's hospitality while they await my pleasure."

His two oldest friends exchanged brief, amused glances before carrying out his orders firmly but peaceably on the astonished delegation. As they mounted and left with the Brytoni escort, Gwenhwyfach discerned varying degrees of consternation wrinkling the visitors' brows.

When she was certain that the Romans—or Visigoths, or whatever in hell they were—could not overhear, Gwenhwyfach asked, "Hostages, Father?"

That brought the briefest of smiles to his lips. "Honored guests, of course." The smile adopted an enigmatic cast. "How long they remain so is another matter altogether."

# TWINS

Yfarryn said, "But what if they send a complaint to their emperor?"

"Think, sister," Gwenhwyfach chided her. "The fastest a message can get to Rome is a month, and that's in good weather." She held up a gloved palm to catch the quickening rain. "Perhaps thrice that length with winter's onset."

"And I shall have reached a decision by then." Their father leaned closer to a chastened-looking Yfarryn. "One of the secrets I've learned over the years is to deal with but one matter at a time." He looked skyward, expression grim. "If God so wills it."

Arthur gave the order for the rest of the burial detail to mount up. Abbot Dafydd's acolytes helped the aging man onto the bench of the empty bier, and the driver maneuvered the dray horse for the tricky descent from the summit of St. Padraic's Isle. Already the tide was washing higher through the tiny strait separating it from the Isle of Maun, signaling it was well past time to leave.

Her father wheeled his stallion around to face the tomb. His features, chiseled by decades of duty to kin and country, were impossible to read. He drew Caleberyllus, held its flat to his face, extended it toward Gyan's grave for several long moments, sheathed it, and ordered the party to depart the islet.

To Gwenhwyfach's surprise, the mourners who had lined the ten-mile road to Port Dhoo-Glass had tripled in number and were clustered along the beach to meet them. People of all ages and classes eddied about the High King and his escort, some bearing gifts and others giving their tears. Most placed their food and flowers and handiwork on the empty bier. Someone stepped up to press a sheathed dagger into Gwenhwyfach's hand. A child gave Yfarryn a cloth doll, which she accepted with a wavering smile. Others came forward to touch a royal cloak hem. Gwenhwyfach received as many salutes as waves, each gesture offered out of love and respect, and she appreciated them all.

Arthur, as was proper, received the most attention. Unlike their journey to the mausoleum, when the soldiers had been under strict orders to hold the crowd at bay, this time he denied no one, from the tiniest child to the most age-withered crone. Often her father took extra moments to console someone who seemed distraught, which seemed backward to Gwenhwyfach. Despite the friction and crises during their three-decades-long marriage, her parents had been as closely bonded as two souls ever could be. By all rights, everyone should have been comforting Arthur. And yet, while he had lost his wife, the people had lost their High Queen, who together with the High King had represented their hopes for the future.

Some of that future had died with her.

With a wrenching pain in her heart, Gwenhwyfach realized that the same was true for the High Queen's daughters. Gyan's death had killed the twins' hopes that their futures would hold even a hint of joy.

Arthur ordered the crowd to stand back. While the escort moved to enforce his command, he dismounted and requested that Medraut and Yfarryn do the same. A pit formed in Gwenhwyfach's stomach. Medraut, looking so handsome in his amber-and-forest-green Clan Lothian tunic, leggings, and cloak, approached with a grin on his face that Gwenhwyfach knew with painful certainty was not meant for her.

Yfarryn moved as one in a dream to obey Arthur's command to stand beside Medraut. Arthur joined her hand to Medraut's as he announced their betrothal and wedding on All Saints', not a month hence.

Gwenhwyfach ached to protest the wrongness of the decision. Never mind the political implications; Gyan never would have consented. As Argyll's àrd-banoigin, the woman through whom the clan's line of succession was determined—though the Christian priests had forbidden her from receiving the clan's mark to indicate this status—Yfarryn possessed the legal right to choose her mate. She cared naught for Medraut. Gwenhwyfach did, but she was second born. Medraut never

would consent to give up the prize Arthur had awarded him.
*Unless...*
Gwenhwyfach stared at her twin, thinking.

THE TANGY sea breeze wafted across Yfarryn's face, and she pulled her cloak's hood tighter about her as she hurried between Port Dhoo-Glass's salt-worn wharfside buildings. Bursts of muted raucous laughter told her she was near her destination, and she withdrew into the shadows of an alley to wait.

Her timing proved good. After two sets of patrons left, singing and staggering arm in arm without a backward glance, the next to emerge from the tavern was a lone man of medium height. He paused in the doorway and glanced around. With the tavern's light at his back, his face was in shadow, but Yfarryn would have known that broad-shouldered, slim-hipped form anywhere.

She blew the three-note signal that only one man would recognize. Lannchu whipped his head around and strode toward her position.

"Yfarryn," he said in a harsh whisper. "What in God's name are you doing out here at this hour? It's too dangerous."

She stepped closer to lay her cheek against his chest, reveling in the rhythm of his heart as his arms closed about her. "Not anymore." Laughter, followed by suspicious-sounding crashes and thuds, reminded her that this was a poor trysting place. She grasped his hand. "Please walk with me."

As they started down the alley, another group of men stumbled from the tavern, swearing loud, drunken oaths of revenge. Lannchu glanced at them, his hand tightening on hers. "Ha. As if I'd go anywhere else." They quickened their pace toward the wharves. "How did you know where to find me?"

Yfarryn gave a low chuckle. "My father isn't the only one

with a stable of spies. But this tip was a waste of my resources." She gave him a frank look. "It took no brain power to guess where you'd be—though you do seem sober enough."

"Too sober." By this time they had reached the water's edge. The tide was out and the wharf's pilings rose beside them like columns of a temple. "Where did you expect me to drown my sorrows?" He gestured toward the restless waters. "Out there?"

She recalled the story he'd once told her, about his father as a young man having contemplated that very act, and she shuddered.

"No." The word barely rose above the hiss of the surf, and she lowered her gaze to the sand. A thousand more words petitioned her tongue for release, but she had no idea where to start. She felt his fingertips slip under her chin, and she did not resist the unspoken suggestion. His gaze was dark with desire, igniting her own. "Lannchu, I cannot imagine a world without you in it." She reached up to touch his cheek. Placing his hand over hers, he leaned into her caress.

"Nor I you, mo ghaolag." *My little love.* Yfarryn never tired of hearing that Caledonaiche endearment from him. He lifted her hand to his lips to bestow a lingering kiss. "No matter whom you must marry."

Images came unbidden of a wedding night spent in Medraut's arms. She tensed. This would be her last chance to be alone with the man she loved, and the realization prompted her to take action she hoped neither of them would regret. She wrapped both arms around his neck and sought his lips with hers. He crushed her to him with startling force, thrusting his tongue into her mouth to probe its secrets. Too soon, he shifted his focus to her chin, her throat, her neck, each kiss torturing her with promises that could never be kept. A raw blend of pleasure and pain forced a moan from her lips.

"It would be best to remain a virgin for your wedding night," said a new voice.

With a startled cry, Yfarryn straightened and looked about.

Hand to dagger, Lannchu whirled. When the intruder stepped from behind a nearby piling, Lannchu folded his arms.

"Fach." Yfarryn didn't care how her sister had found them; the pertinent question was why. "Don't expect me to bid you well come, because you aren't."

Fach tossed her braids, uttering a light chuckle when Yfarryn deepened her scowl. "Not even if I were to give you the solution to your dilemma?"

"What would you do? Guard our backs as we run away?" A romantic notion, but not a feasible one. "Father would kill us all. If Medraut didn't find us first."

"You're right. My plan is simpler." She extended her open-palmed hand. "We trade places."

Astonishment forced Yfarryn back a pace. "What? You're mad, Gwenhwyfach. Mother's death has addled your wits."

"You're the one who's not thinking," Fach growled. "If I marry Medraut in your stead, you'll be free to enjoy more dalliances with him." She jerked her head in Lannchu's direction. "Though heaven only knows why."

His posture tensed, but he remained silent. Yfarryn shot him an appreciative glance before leveling her gaze on her daft sister. "Even without the Argyll clan-mark on my forearm, this plan of yours won't work. I'm much better at wielding distaff and ladle than dagger and sword. We'd be discovered before the wedding feast grew cold."

Fach tapped her chin. "That could present a problem..."

Still, the idea had merit, and Yfarryn set her mind to salvaging it. "Not if we spent from now until the wedding always in each other's company."

"Doing what?" Lannchu said to Yfarryn. "Gwenhwyfach is an accomplished warrior. The most you could hope to learn from her in three weeks is the basic moves. That would never fool anyone."

"Yet it might be enough," Fach said. "Especially if you, sister, can teach me how to run a large household, which you handle so well."

"Perhaps." Planting hands on hips, Yfarryn regarded her sister. "But why would you do this for me? Why tie yourself to a man you don't want so I can be free?"

Fach grinned. "That's just it. I do want Medraut. If I can prove myself an ardent lover, then when our trick is discovered, it shouldn't matter."

Yfarryn felt her jaw slacken. She began to ask what interest a man a score of years her senior could possibly hold for Fach but decided she didn't want to know. The important thing was that Fach was willing to try this absurd stunt and believed it would work.

"We'll have to invent a suitable explanation for why we're spending so much time together," Yfarryn pointed out.

"Easy," her sister said. "We'll just tell everyone that since we grew up apart, we wish to spend as much time together as possible before we're forced to part again."

"Very well." Yfarryn linked arms with Lannchu in preparation for the return walk, already forming ideas about how to educate Fach in the domestic arts. "Then I propose we begin right away."

## Chapter 2
### The Actions

Back home at Caer Lugubalion, Arthur's fortress at the western end of Hadrian's Wall and headquarters of the Dragon Legion, the twins set their plan into motion. They ate, rode, hunted, fought, and worked together. They adopted similar hairstyles and modes of dress. Even in speech and gestures they became more alike as they taught each other the nuances of their different worlds.

If anyone noticed this unusual behavior, they held their tongues. The sisters surmised that everyone else was too wrapped up in either grief or preparations for the imminent wedding to question them about it.

The days flew by in a blur, and the lessons did not come easily to either twin. Yfarryn's strength would never come close to Gwenhwyfach's, no matter how much weaponry skill she managed to attain. And Gwenhwyfach, possessing no interest in domestic affairs, could not hope to become Yfarryn's equal in that regard. Yet they made progress and talked late into the night to devise ways to disguise the weaknesses in their scheme.

With All Saints' a few days away, it was only natural for Gwenhwyfach to insist upon being part of Yfarryn's escort to Medraut's fortress at Dun Eidyn, fourscore miles to the north, on the eastern end of the Antonine Wall. Arthur not only approved Gwenhwyfach's request but encouraged it, pleased by his daughters' developing friendship.

No one suspected that the smiling young woman entering Dun Eidyn's gates wearing the Clan Argyll mantle of leadership over her midnight-blue gown was not Gwenhwyfar nic Gyanhumara but Gwenhwyfach ferch Arthur. Medraut greeted the woman he thought was his bride with a deep bow and a lavish kiss on the back of her hand.

Gwenhwyfach giggled demurely. It wasn't an act.

She and her sister continued being inseparable as they scouted the kitchens, training grounds, servants' quarters, armory, and other areas of the fortress. By mutual agreement, they dressed similarly but not identically, lest someone suspect their plan.

The wedding day arrived in full autumnal splendor. Although Gwenhwyfach and Yfarryn remained closeted together for the final hours, there were too many maidservants about to risk imparting any more instructions to each other. Still, Gwenhwyfach felt confident that she could maintain the ruse long enough to win Medraut's heart.

With more than her share of a bride's nervousness, Gwenhwyfach stood at Medraut's side in Dun Eidyn's chapel before God and Arthur and the most important nobles of Brydein and Caledonia. The ceremonial kiss Medraut bestowed upon her was deep and satisfying. She permitted herself the luxury of a small smile she hoped didn't appear too triumphant.

# TWINS

Seated near one end of the high table with her father and cousins, and ever so thankful not to be the center of attention, Yfarryn studied the newly married couple. Fach seemed to be playing the part of the blushing virgin bride well, keeping her gaze downcast and her voice soft.

Yfarryn searched the feast hall for the man for whom she had agreed to this deception. He was sitting beside his parents at a table close to the dais, and she tried not to look too long at him. Gwenhwyfach ferch Arthur would not have given Lannchu a moment's thought, and Yfarryn's performance was just as vital for maintaining the illusion. The temptation was too great to resist altogether, but she curbed it as best she could, forming a plan for slipping him a message so they could meet later this night.

In one of those odd silences that occurs during public gatherings, Yfarryn heard Medraut say, "My wife, this is a fine feast. Did you oversee the preparations yourself?"

Yfarryn turned her head as fast as she dared, wondering how her sister would respond. Fach looked startled, like a cornered deer.

"Ah—no, my lord husband. I did not." Fach indicated her appearance in a feminine gesture. "I was too busy with my own preparations, of course." Yfarryn gave silent applause to her sister's wit. "But I do look forward to assuming this duty when I become better accustomed to my new surroundings."

"Well spoken, my dear. I look forward to it too." Medraut leaned over to give his bride a kiss.

After he straightened and buried his face in his tankard, Yfarryn and Fach exchanged glances laden with relief.

SNATCHES OF drunken singing and ribald jokes and coarse laughter in the corridor alerted Gwenhwyfach that her bridegroom was approaching. Her maids glanced toward the sounds and burst into fits of giggles, which Gwenhwyfach tried her best to match, knowing it was what her sister would have done. She dismissed them with a word of thanks. Outside, the men started an off-key rendition of a crude marching song about a mercenary warrior whose travels could be followed by the ages of the flame-haired children at inns where he had stayed. As the last of her maids slipped, blushing, from the bedchamber, closing the door behind her, Gwenhwyfach resisted the urge to hum along.

She surveyed the bed, with its lavender-scented linens and lamb's-wool blankets, debating whether to shed her embroidered sleeping tunic and climb into bed.

No. Yfarryn would not have appeared eager.

Gwenhwyfach wrapped her cloak about her and selected a chair near the fire in full view of the door.

The giggles of the maids in the outer chamber escalated. Medraut murmured something in that appealing voice of his that Gwenhwyfach couldn't make out. Another brief fit of giggles heralded the banging of the outer door and abrupt silence.

The bedchamber door opened. A dragon writhed in her stomach. This was the moment upon which all her plans hinged.

Gwenhwyfach summoned a nervous smile for her bridegroom that wasn't feigned.

Medraut flicked his gaze about the chamber before letting it come to rest upon his bride. "You've become more like your sister." His speech was only a wee bit slurred. The dragon in Gwenhwyfach's stomach took a leap. He waved a hand in her direction. "Chosen like a true warrior."

He was right, Gwenhwyfach realized with a mental groan. Defensively, the room offered two possibilities: near the door for the greatest element of surprise, and near the fire, with a wall to guard her back and a weapon nearby in the form of the

## TWINS

blunt but heavy iron poker.

She rose. "Not so, my lord." She fought to keep her voice low and even, her eyes downcast. "I was cold." She added a shiver and chafed her arms.

"Ah." Gwenhwyfach kept her gaze lowered as Medraut approached her. "Perhaps I can be of assistance."

He unpinned her brooch. The cloak slid from her shoulders to pool at her feet. Gwenhwyfach allowed herself to look up and saw hunger smoldering in her husband's eyes. She tried to forget that his hunger wasn't for her. In time, it would be.

Pulling her close, he fastened his lips to hers. She put up as much resistance as she thought Yfarryn might have done before submitting to Medraut's embrace. His tongue explored the tip of hers as his fingers discovered the tips of her breasts, sending waves of passion coursing through her body. As his fingers worked lower and his tongue thrust deeper, her fight to bridle her passion intensified.

Medraut swept her into his arms, strode to the bed, and laid her down. She couldn't keep her eyes from him as he unbuckled his belt, stripped off his tunic, and loosened the thongs of his trews. Whether Yfarryn would have reacted that way or not, Gwenhwyfach didn't know and didn't care. What mattered was that he was soon to become, irrevocably and irreversibly, hers.

He bent down to untie her tunic, exposing her breasts. She felt the flesh grow taut between his fingers, causing an exquisite ache to flare between her thighs. Closing her eyes, she tilted her head back against the pillows and uttered a soft sigh. His lips covered hers while his hand began a slow quest between her legs, caressing upward. Her body felt engulfed by flame, and she wished it would never end.

Short of his goal, he stopped and raised his head. She opened her eyes to find him regarding her, the hunger in his eyes undiminished. She shifted her hips provocatively. His hand remained still, but a languid smile formed on his lips. "Does this mean, Gwenhwyfar nic Gyanhumara, that I just might be able to teach you to love me?"

"Please call me Yfarryn." Gwenhwyfach ferch Arthur flashed what she hoped was an inviting smile. "My lord husband may teach me anything." She pulled his face to hers and whispered, "Please teach me… everything."

It was an offer that, to her boundless delight, Medraut map Loth wasted no time to accept.

CLUTCHING HER hood, Yfarryn scurried from shadow to shadow toward the stables, hoping her flame-red hair would not betray her. The few individuals she encountered after leaving the feast hall were too far gone in their revelry to pay her any heed. After sighting her destination and slipping into its horsey warmth, she breathed a swift prayer of thanks.

She groped her way from stall to stall, whistling the signal. Unbidden came the thought of how Fach was faring, but Yfarryn submerged her curiosity. If all were not well in the nuptial chamber, then the inevitable hue and cry would be raised for her, Yfarryn, as well.

Best not to entertain such thoughts when the object of her heart's desire lay so close, if she could discover where he was hiding.

Since the only sounds to reach her ears were the restless shuffling and snorting of the horses and, from much farther away, the muted but rowdy noises emanating from the feast hall, Yfarryn dared a louder whistle. Near the ladder leading up to the loft, she was rewarded with a soft but rhythmic tapping. Glancing at the wisps of hay dangling from between the rough planking overhead, she smiled, moved to the base of the ladder, shed her cloak, and began the wobbly ascent.

As she concentrated on attaining each rung, her course grew easier. She looked up to see Lannchu gripping the top of the ladder, a grin splitting his face. She felt her cheeks heat.

From his angle, he had a more than ample view down the top of her gown. A tingling rush swept through her body with the realization that soon he'd have a more than ample view of the rest of her.

He assisted her into the loft, his hands lingering on her waist as she stood facing him. The combination of the climb's exertion and the need to remain stealthy—not to mention anticipation of the exertion to come—left Yfarryn breathless. The moon cast striped shadows through the timbers of the loft's siding. She felt acutely conscious of Lannchu's eager gaze upon her, the rapid rise and fall of her bosom, and the hammering of her heart.

Years of Christian moral training warred with her desire, and she entertained the thought of making an excuse to leave. Despite the convention of her mother's people and Lannchu's dictating that sexual union forged a marriage, rather than the other way around, Yfarryn believed her relations with him could not be considered pure and right unless she wed him, blessed by the Church. If word of her conduct were to become public, she would bring shame and dishonor not only upon herself but her father too.

Worse still, the secret of her switch with Fach would be revealed. It was common knowledge that the real Gwenhwyfach would never consort with Lannchu.

And yet, there he stood, looking handsome in his simple stable hand's guise, with stray bits of hay sticking out at odd angles from his hair, his shoulders, his chest... without thinking, she reached up to brush one away. He captured her hand and lifted it to his lips. The kiss he planted there was warm and moist. He nibbled a knuckle and she giggled. The hay and horses mingled with the ale lingering on his breath created an intoxicating aroma she couldn't resist. To the devil with purity, she decided, and caressed his quickening tòn. His breath caught, and his grin widened.

He released her hand, picked her up, kissed her soundly, and deposited her on a mound of hay overspread with his cloak. The fragrant hay made a crunching sound, and her heart clenched with the thought that they might be overheard. She gasped.

Lannchu eased down beside her. "Fear not, mo ghaolag," he whispered. "We are quite alone." Below, a horse nickered. He smiled. "And their rumors won't betray us, I promise."

Yfarryn hoped not. She had a hard enough time trying not to imagine the possibility of someone entering the stables to find out why the horses were so restless.

With sword-callused fingertips, he traced a line across her cheek, down her throat, and on to the stays of her bodice. While his lips covered hers, his fingers loosened the thongs. As the last loop came undone, she felt her breasts surge free. Her remaining inhibitions took flight. He pulled her into a sitting position and lifted off her undertunic. She glimpsed his smile of sheer appreciation as he laid her back down and lowered his mouth first to one breast, then its twin. Lips parted, she arched her head back as an aching tightness burned between her legs.

Feeling she had to do something, anything to help bring her desire to fruition, she reached for the edges of his tunic and tried to work it off his chest. He halted his assault on her breasts to comply with her unspoken demand. She placed a palm on his chest and was rewarded by the sleek feel of his muscles, covered with a fine layer of hair. She moved her hand down over the flat of his belly and found the laces of his trews. Her breathing quickened, punctuated by the quickening rhythm of her heart, as she untied the thongs and began sliding the garment over his hips before realizing her reach was too short. He stood to finish the task she had begun.

The hay crunched again as he lay down beside her. His hand drifted across her breasts, coaxing the nipples to hardness. He shifted, and she felt his ready tòn pressing against her thigh. "Are you sure this is what you want, mo ghaolag?"

She couldn't see him well, but from his tone she could imagine the concern that must be dominating his expression, and it made her love him all the more. Again the ache stabbed her groin. This time she understood. It was the pain of aloneness, of unfulfilled passion, of unconsummated love. Her virginity, the core of her inmost self, was the greatest gift she could offer any man. She could not withhold it from the one man she would ever love. Even if her father betrothed her to someone else, she, Gwenhwyfar nic Gyanhumara, would invoke Caledonian custom to choose her husband, if only for this night.

And to the devil with the consequences.

"Yes, my love." As he moved into position for the fulfillment of both their desires, she added, "Mo leannan."

*My beloved husband.*

## Chapter 3

## The Fears

Scarcely leaving Medraut's side all day, Gwenhwyfach reveled in her new status. At the horse races, the fair, the mock combat demonstrations—in which she yearned to be a participant—everywhere, she was treated with honor and respect. She knew she had to enjoy the attention while it lasted; once the nuptials were over, the real work as Medraut's wife would begin.

That evening, seated on the dais in the feast hall between her husband and father, she scanned the crowd, running a fingertip along one side of her gown's neckline and wishing her sister had preferred a style that was less revealing. Lannchu seemed at ease, chortling at the jests making the rounds at the bachelors' table. When Gwenhwyfach caught him glancing up at the dais, she was not surprised to note that his gaze had lost its usual haunted quality. Yfarryn, seated on the other side of Arthur, was looking downright smug.

# TWINS

If Gwenhwyfach interpreted that wordless exchange correctly, they had become lovers last night. Inwardly, she cheered.

Arthur too seemed to be in an expansive mood as he traded quips and snatches of songs with everyone at the high table and downed more wine than Gwenhwyfach had seen him imbibe in years. If his grief for Gyan's passing, which had been evident during the days of his self-imposed seclusion following the funeral, was not altogether gone, the wedding festivities appeared to be helping him to forget it.

Without warning, he crashed his fist to the tabletop and stood. Silence reigned.

"My lords and ladies... my dearest friends. It pleases me beyond measure to see my eldest daughter"—Arthur smiled at Gwenhwyfach, and she prayed that her answering smile didn't look as uneasy as it felt—"safely and contentedly wed." He bent to retrieve his goblet, raised it toward Medraut and Gwenhwyfach, tipped it to his lips, and drank. The rest of the company followed his example. Arthur went on, "Gwenhwyfar and Medraut will make a fine team." He took another swallow. "As coregents in my absence."

"What?" Gwenhwyfach felt as though she'd been stabbed. She twisted to look up at him. "Your absence?" The question was amplified by most people throughout the hall.

Arthur nodded, as much to the assembly as to his daughter. Voice still pitched to reach the hall's farthest corners, he said, "If anyone has forgotten the threat made to the sovereignty of Brydein by the self-styled Emperor of Rome less than one month ago, I have not. Our troop strength stands at the highest level ever, with no outlet for their skills since the Lord has seen fit to grant peace within Brydein's shores. I propose"—he was obliged to raise his voice over the escalating murmurs—"that we take this insult to Lucius's doorstep and shove it down his barbaric throat!"

The response was loud and instantaneous, but not unanimous. A few dissenting voices struggled to be heard. Bedwyr argued that an invasion of Rome would take weeks to organize, followed by a long and bloody campaign across Gaul, in spite of the support of the Franks already on friendly terms with Brydein, just to reach their final destination. Not to mention the force that would greet them once they arrived.

Privately, Gwenhwyfach agreed with Bedwyr. That her father, renowned for his thorough evaluation of risks versus benefits prior to embarking upon any military action, would even contemplate such an expensive and foolhardy foray defied belief, even with the imperial purple as a potential prize. She studied Arthur as he permitted his followers to have their say, searching for signs that the drink had planted this idea. But his stance was steady, as were his grip on the goblet and set of his jaw and resolve in his gaze.

"And the Roman ambassadors, Your Majesty?" Gawain asked.

"We cannot risk their getting wind of this operation and warning their master." Arthur turned to Cai. "Kill them." The coldness in his tone could have frozen the sun.

This prompted a round of cheers and speeches rife with themes of outrage toward Rome and loyalty toward king and country. Loudest among them was Angusel of Caledonia. In ringing tones, he lauded the High King's decision and exhorted his peers to action. Ensnared by his frenzied rhetoric, Gwenhwyfach fought the temptation of leaping to her feet to pledge her sword to her father's cause.

As "Gwenhwyfar," she had no sword to pledge.

She gripped Medraut's hand, hoping to retain her grip on reality as the dragon went on the prowl in her gut. Her husband favored her with a grin, no doubt pleased that Arthur had appointed him coregent. *And I am coregent, but not as a warrior...* her inner dragon's pacing intensified. When Arthur announced that "Gwenhwyfach" would remain at Caer Lugubalion to oversee Brydein's defenses, the dragon began turning somersaults.

Gwenhwyfach caught her sister's gaze. Yfarryn looked

pale and shaken. Gwenhwyfach felt her ire rise. Her sister's cowardice was going to ruin everything.

---

YFARRYN ENVIED her sister's courage in the face of the overwhelming odds. Fach looked like their mother incarnate, standing proud and unyielding near the hearth in Yfarryn's chambers while she, Yfarryn, traversed the floor, wringing her hands.

"We must change places!" Yfarryn stopped before Fach to gesture imploringly. "Don't you see the dangers? With Father and Lannchu and Gawain and the others gone—"

"Any support we might have garnered in the event of our discovery leaves with them." Fach crossed her arms. "But I will not give up my husband." Malicious disdain dominated her expression. "Are you so willing to give up Lannchu?"

Yfarryn gritted her teeth as she studied the ceiling timbers, willing her sister to understand. "If it is for the good of Brydein"—she leveled her gaze at Fach—"then, yes. Yes, I am."

Fach snorted. "Fine words." She turned to pick up the poker and jabbed the dying embers. "For a coward."

An inarticulate sound lodged in Yfarryn's throat. *Coward? How dare she!* "And you're a selfish whore!"

Fach faced her, grinning. "My marriage was sanctified by the Church. Was yours?"

Yfarryn felt her face burn less from the accusation than from the memory of Lannchu's ardor. It strengthened her resolve. "Your marriage, Gwenhwyfach ferch Arthur, is a lie."

Her sister's head jerked as if she'd been slapped. She dropped the poker with a clatter and shouldered past Yfarryn. At the door, she paused and turned, her face contorted with contempt. "I'd rather live with a pleasurable lie than the miserable truth."

The miserable truth, Yfarryn realized as the door slammed

shut behind her sister, was going to condemn them all.

# Chapter 4
## The Reactions

AS AUTUMN YIELDED to winter's onslaught, Gwenhwyfach strove to be the wife Medraut expected her to be. She took command of the servants in the only manner she knew, as though they were a military unit. After spending a few weeks of adjusting to her expectations, the servants began accomplishing their tasks with admirable precision and efficiency. Perhaps not with the same creative flair Yfarryn would have elicited, such as the procurement of rare foods and the unusual presentations of more common fare. Whatever deficiencies Gwenhwyfach perceived in the performance of her domestic duties, she tried to make up for in the bedchamber.

So far, Medraut wasn't complaining.

But he didn't seem to be growing as close to her as she had hoped he would, a fact evidenced by his insistence upon calling her "Gwenhwyfar" rather than "Yfarryn."

However, the distance between them never felt wider than

during Medraut's sessions with his advisers as he planned for his imminent regency. *Coregency*, she reminded him, which gave her as much right to be present as anyone. Unable to deny her logic, he would allow her to remain. Whenever she heard the latest word of her father's invasion preparations, it made her miss her home and her old life. But invariably Medraut would ask her to look into another task—a special cloak he'd commissioned, the status of siege provisions, or the like—and she knew she had been dismissed.

These times disturbed her more profoundly than her enforced inability to practice the warriors' arts.

Gwenhwyfach wished for some way to unburden her soul. Confiding in Dun Eidyn's priest, whom she barely knew, was out of the question. And she realized, too late, that her handling of the servants prevented her from forging a deeper relationship with them.

On the calends of April, Gwenhwyfach stood at her husband's side to bid farewell and Godspeed to Arthur and the departing army. Remarkable by her absence was Yfarryn, who had sent word that illness prevented her from attending. Gwenhwyfach wondered how much of her sister's illness was attributed to their argument. That memory had haunted her through many sleepless nights. While Gwenhwyfach preferred to think of her decision to perpetuate the ruse as optimistic rather than selfish, she had to admit that Yfarryn's words had held a grain of truth. Standing on the dock as her father's ships disappeared across the sea, Gwenhwyfach resolved to make amends.

The problem was she didn't know how to begin.

An opportunity presented itself a few days later, when Medraut requested that his wife host a sumptuous feast in honor of their coregency. It was a fine idea, but Gwenhwyfach knew she would need her sister's help. She poured out her thoughts and pleas into a letter she hoped would soften Yfarryn's heart, but she was not sure how well she had succeeded. After the courier departed her chambers with the sealed message, Gwenhwyfach began making plans for the feast in the event her sister refused to come.

Yfarryn didn't even acknowledge Gwenhwyfach's missive. Saddened beyond measure, Gwenhwyfach struggled through the last stage of the preparations as best she could.

"You call this a king's feast?" Medraut roared at her that evening, swiping his trencher from the table.

Food and implements flew everywhere. Gwenhwyfach caught his meat knife before it could graze her cheek. The feast hall became tomb silent. She felt everyone's gaze upon her as her mortification grew. Willing her heart to slow, she laid down the knife. "I am truly sorry, my lord, if my best efforts do not please you."

"Indeed." Medraut looked first at the knife, then at her. "A pity you are not as deft with cooking utensils as your are with weapons, Gwenhwyfar." A predatory grin spread across his face. "Or should I call you Gwenhwyfach?"

"What? No! I-I don't know what—"

"Save your lies." Medraut reached into his tunic and withdrew a sheet of parchment, folded exactly as Gwenhwyfach had remembered doing it a week ago. The seal, she observed with mounting queasiness, was broken. "Explain this." The parchment rattled as he waved it before her face.

A quick scan of the crowd revealed many puzzled faces, and more than a few hostile ones, but no supporters.

Sighing, she bowed her head. "It's true. Gwenhwyfar and I exchanged places."

Over the surprised murmurs of the other feasters, Medraut said, "At Arthur's command, I'll wager."

"No!" Shock forced her to her feet, fists knotted. Her chair crashed onto the platform behind her. "No. My father had nothing to do with this. He doesn't even know."

Incredulity replaced anger on Medraut's face. "You're asking me to believe that a father cannot tell apart his own children?"

Gwenhwyfach's mind raced to form explanations. It hadn't

occurred to her to question Arthur's failure to notice the switch, only to be thankful of her good fortune. "Perhaps he was blinded by grief? Preoccupied by invasion plans?"

"Irrelevant." Medraut rose to face Gwenhwyfach, making her wish for a sword to keep him at bay. "The High King is responsible for the actions of peasant and princess alike. Brydein needs a new High King, one capable of keeping his wits about him." Medraut's tone froze her soul. He grabbed her arm and yanked her close. The ale on his breath made her stomach churn. "What I want to know, Gwenhwyfach ferch Arthur, is why you thought you could get away with this deceit."

"Because…" Pain bolted through her arm where his fingers dug in. She bit her lip, fighting down the panic that rose with the bile in her throat. Bowing her head, she dropped her voice to a whisper. "Because I love you."

"Love?" Medraut's laugh was an ugly sound. "What love is built on manipulation and lies?" When she didn't respond, he released her arm, grabbed her chin, and forced her head up. His expression of smoldering rage frightened her more than a hundred armed enemies ever could. "Not a love I want any part of, Gwenhwyfach. You may be certain of that."

He thrust her into the hands of a guard and ordered him to lock her up and stand watch, and to permit no visitors except someone to clean and deliver food. Medraut needn't have worried, she thought as the guard escorted her from the hall. Through her own foolishness, she had left herself no one at Dun Eidyn to whom she could turn.

The last thing she heard before the feast hall doors thundered shut behind them was Medraut urging his followers to join their new High King in paying a visit upon the woman who should have become his wife.

His tone chilled her soul.

# TWINS

SEATED BEHIND her father's desk in his workroom in the praetorium of Caer Lugubalion, and feeling unqualified for the task, Yfarryn tried to make sense of the scouting report. An army, led by Medraut, was headed her way at a pace that would put them at her gates by midafternoon.

Something at Dun Eidyn had to have gone terribly wrong, she surmised with mounting dread; Fach would have sent a warning. Or was she still angry about what she had perceived in Yfarryn as cowardice?

That Yfarryn had received no communication from her sister since the wedding confirmed the awful truth.

Hoping Medraut was just drilling troops in her corner of Brydein, Yfarryn stood, smoothed her robes, ordered her aide to open the fort's gates, and prepared to meet Brydein's coregent in the praetorium's judgment hall.

He swaggered in, armed for battle and escorted by a score of his highest-ranking officers. None had drawn weapons, but they looked menacing enough. Yfarryn repressed her fear, gripped the curved arms of her backless chair, sucked in a breath, and prayed for a miracle.

"My lord regent." She swallowed, fighting to keep her voice steady. "To what do I owe the honor of this visit?"

His grin did little to alleviate her concern. "Your Highness, my men and I are hungry, and I thought you might be willing to provision us." He swept her a courtly bow.

*Hungry?* In spite of her sinking spirits, she resolved to make light of the situation. "Certainly, my lord, you are welcome to all we have." Smiling, she made an expansive gesture. "Although I'm afraid it won't be as well prepared as you're accustomed to from your wife's skills."

Rage seared away Medraut's grin. He stalked toward Yfarryn, cocked his hand, and smote her so hard that she toppled backward off the chair. The force of her fall knocked the breath from her, cutting off her outcry. Her head spun, and her cheek burned from his blow. Rough hands seized her arms, hauling her to her feet.

When she dared to look, Medraut was holding his sword toward her, hilt first. "Care to avenge the insult, Your Highness?" Yfarryn could only stare in horror at the gleaming blade, knowing it would be useless in her hands against a warrior of his renown. "I thought not." He flipped the sword, caught it by the hilt, and leveled the point at her. "I do not tolerate lies, Gwenhwyfar nic Gyanhumara." Though addressing the guard, Medraut glared at Yfarryn as he said, "Escort Her Highness to her chambers and see to it she doesn't leave. I will visit at my leisure to claim what should have been mine months ago."

His arrogance ignited her ire. "You're too late, my lord." Hands on hips, she arched her back, revealing through the robes the bulge of her womb.

Medraut's laugh was harsh. "As High King, I shall claim Lannchu's brat is mine, and not one person in Brydein will dare to disagree." He pressed the sword's point to her belly. "Least of all you."

"Come, now, nephew," purred a new voice. "Is that any way to treat the mother of your heir?" Yfarryn felt her jaw slacken as Arthur's sister, Morghe, glided into the hall, lavishly gowned and adorned with jewels.

Medraut must have noticed Yfarryn's surprise, for his grin returned. He sheathed his sword, and Morghe linked her arm with his. "Permit me to introduce you to your new High Queen."

"What!"

Morghe wagged a finger. "It's not what you think, my dear. Our relationship is"—she gazed up at Medraut and winked—"purely political. Dalriada's troops in exchange for the crown." She gave Yfarryn a frank appraisal. "It appears that I'm not the only one who knows how to get what she wants." Her scornful laughter stung Yfarryn's ears. "But I, at least, know how to keep it."

As Medraut's officer ushered Yfarryn from the hall, she devised a plan for getting a message to her father and prayed she could find a way to make it work.

IMPRISONED IN her quarters in Dun Eidyn, Gwenhwyfach struggled to keep from going mad. Contact with others was limited to the guards, who never entered her chambers, and one taciturn female servant tasked with delivering her meals and seeing to her cleaning needs. The woman seldom glanced at Gwenhwyfach as she worked, and never spoke. Gwenhwyfach didn't even know her name.

To combat the rampant boredom, she devised exercises with the poker and firewood and practiced them with a vengeance, fantasizing about using these crude weapons to overpower her guards and escape, perhaps disguised as the servant woman. But escape to where? With all of Dun Eidyn against her, and perhaps most of the folk of the surrounding countryside too, her chances of finding sanctuary lay somewhere between slim and none.

The solitary imprisonment lasted for week after dreary week... which explained why, when the noises began, she was slow to identify the reason for the prolonged shouts, the pounding of many feet, and the clatter of arms.

*Battle?* Gwenhwyfach shook her head, certain she was dreaming. A glance out the chamber's window told her she was not. Scores of warships clogged the harbor. Gwenhwyfach squinted at the scene, scrubbed a hand over her eyes, and looked again. The warships were flying the Scarlet Dragon!

Despite the inevitability of having to explain why she had married Medraut in Yfarryn's stead, she had never felt more relieved in her life. And yet, when Arthur burst into her chamber, his armor and sword streaked with blood and his eyes blazing as if ready to shoot thunderbolts, all Gwenhwyfach could do was collapse into a sobbing, repentant heap at his feet.

The clink of metal and creak of leather told her he had sheathed his sword and knelt, and she felt his hand upon her head. "Gwenhwyfach." The gentle concern in his tone wrenched more sobs from her throat. He pressed her head to his chest and circled his arms about her. "Gwenhwyfach, what happened? Why are you imprisoned here? Where is Gwenhwyfar? Why did I get a message from her that Medraut has attacked Caer Lugubalion?"

*Oh, merciful God in heaven. Why, indeed?*

Pulling free of her father's embrace, she drew a deep breath, repaired the rags of her composure, and told him everything she knew.

After she had finished and answered his questions as best she could, he knelt for a long time, staring up at the ceiling. His thoughts she could only guess. None were promising. He stood, held out his hand, and helped her rise. Her stomach clenched in anticipation of his judgment.

"Prepare to ride with me and my men," was all he said.

"What?"

He gave her an annoyed look. "You heard me, daughter. I'll need your help. It's been only a few weeks. Medraut is likely still trying to build his power base. If we can get to him before he turns enough men to his cause, there's a good chance we can set things to rights without more bloodshed."

"More?" Staring at the dried blood on his breastplate, she felt foolish for having asked the obvious.

"Dun Eidyn's defenders resisted my landing. My casualties were minimal, but I lost an officer." Arthur's gaze grew distant, and he sighed. "Since it's so close, and I must await the arrival of the infantry from the Continent, I've given Angusel leave to take his body home to Senaudon."

"Oh, God, not—" Gwenhwyfach covered her mouth. "Lannchu?"

He nodded, sternness dominating his expression. "Your foolishness and your sister's have brought this situation upon Brydein. Pray that his death, and the deaths of the others who

# TWINS

fell here today, is the only price we must pay for it."

Blinking back tears for the irony and magnitude of Lannchu's sacrifice, Gwenhwyfach carried out the High King's command as fervently as she knew how.

Three days later, Chieftain Angusel returned from Senaudon. The foot soldiers, led by Cai, had arrived the day before. The grueling pace, coupled with a storm during their voyage, had left most of the men too sick for another forced march. Never in her life had Gwenhwyfach seen Angusel urge Arthur to action with more vehemence. Even though Arthur had planned to wait until the bulk of his force recovered, at last he yielded to Angusel's entreaty. Arthur assembled the cavalry for departure, outlined his plans to head for Camboglanna, and ordered Cai to bring up the rear with the infantry at best possible speed.

Gwenhwyfach was only too glad to put the walls of Dun Eidyn, perched atop its saddle-shaped summit, far behind her.

With frequent changing of mounts for remounts, and infrequent ration stops, Arthur's advance force made the three-day journey in two. They encountered little resistance along the way, but picked up little support either. Medraut had been thorough in garnering both men and materiel on his way to Caer Lugubalion, and Arthur's men were obliged to forage for game and fodder. Citizens expressing the desire to fight for Arthur he welcomed, especially those owning horses. The rest he instructed to join the infantry when it arrived.

They reached the old Roman fortress of Camboglanna, on the crooked bank of the Atan, expecting a fight but finding the garrison deserted. Gwenhwyfach surmised Medraut was staging his army nearby at the much larger fortress of Caer Lugubalion. Arthur moved his troops inside and set a defensive perimeter. Gwenhwyfach could guess why: it was only a matter of time before Medraut's patrols discovered their presence and he marshaled his army to attack. She hoped Cai would arrive with the infantry before Medraut could seal off the area.

It was not to be. Gwenhwyfach woke two mornings later to shouts and the pounding of many running feet. She donned her jerkin, breastplate, leggings, and boots, girded on her sword, tucked her helmet under one arm, and joined the men racing for the battlements. What she saw there stole her breath. Medraut's army was arrayed a bowshot's length from the walls, disappearing into the mist-shrouded distance.

Someone pointed and uttered a whoop of triumph. Emerging from the mist to the north was Cai's division. But, as near as Gwenhwyfach could tell, his troops weren't numerous enough to break Medraut's siege. She glanced at her father standing beside her. If she interpreted aright the clenching of his jaw and fists, he had reached the same conclusion. They watched Cai's men halt on a ridge north of Camboglanna, close enough to lend Arthur support if needed but far enough away from Medraut that he didn't feel compelled to attack them yet.

A lone rider carrying a white flag approached Camboglanna's walls from Medraut's camp. "Lord Arthur, Medraut the High King commands a parlay to negotiate the terms of your surrender."

"Never!" shouted Angusel, sword aloft. "Medraut is no more the rightful High King than your mother is."

Arthur gripped Angusel's sword arm and forced it down. "When and where?" he called to the messenger.

"Tomorrow at sun's zenith, my lord, in the shade of yon oak." The man pointed to a massive tree growing where the river had carved out a sharp turn. The proposed location was equidistant from the fortress and the camp.

"Arthur, don't—"

Arthur's glare cut Angusel off. He said to the messenger, "Providing I may bring twelve armed men and Medraut does the same, and that the Bishop of Caer Lugubalion presides, then I agree to this meeting." As the messenger sped toward Medraut's camp, Arthur murmured, gazing heavenward, "And may God have mercy upon us all."

Angusel sheathed his sword and gripped Arthur's arms.

"Are you daft? Medraut is in the wrong. You're under no obligation to do anything he says."

Smiling, he clapped Angusel's shoulders. "I know my obligations, don't fear. And I haven't gone mad yet. But I need to know my options."

"Ha." Angusel let go and folded his arms. "Medraut won't give you any."

"No matter how dire the circumstances, my friend, there are always options." Arthur nodded toward Angusel's sword. "I am counting on you and eleven other men to preserve one of them."

"Men?" Gwenhwyfach asked Arthur. "I'm coming with you."

He rested a hand on her shoulder, his expression kind but firm. "No, daughter. With you in my escort, Medraut may become more difficult to reason with." His fingers tightened and withdrew. "I need you to guard one of my options too, by ordering out the cavalry at the first sign of trouble."

"You expect treachery, Arthur?" Angusel asked.

The High King sighed, glancing at the siege camp. "I'd be a bloody fool not to."

Though she retired shortly after sundown, Gwenhwyfach couldn't sleep. When she did, it was riddled with fitful dreams. The worst was a vision of her mother. Gyan was bristling at all points, like the war goddess Nemetona, with armor that gleamed to rival the sun. Turning to face Gwenhwyfach, arms extended and palms upward, Gyan displayed a beatific smile.

As Gwenhwyfach raised her arms to embrace her mother, she glanced at her own hands. They were dripping blood.

She woke, gasping and shaking. The prospect of returning to sleep was pointless. She rose, armed herself, fastened her cloak in place, and headed for the battlements. The first gray light of dawn was streaking the blue-black sky above the myriad campfires of Medraut's army. Near the oak, a detachment was already erecting the tent for the meeting. Gwenhwyfach watched with morbid fascination as the work progressed, the dragon in her stomach writhing with worry.

By the time Arthur found her, the worry had transformed into outright dread. She wrapped her arms about him. "Father, please don't leave," she whispered.

She felt his hand stroke her head. "I must, Gwenhwyfach, if I am to convince Medraut to forgive you and your sister." His fingers slid under her chin to make her look up. "As I have."

Sobs welled. She choked them back to say, "God be with you, Father." *Even as I cannot be.*

After a final embrace, they parted. Through blurred eyes, Gwenhwyfach watched the Majesty of Brydein descend into the courtyard, mount his stallion, gather his men about him, and ride to meet his destiny.

As arranged, Arthur and his delegation met Medraut's at the oak. The bishop, arms outstretched, intoned a prayer, then beckoned Arthur and Medraut into the tent while their men took wary positions outside.

Since there was nothing further to see, Gwenhwyfach left orders with the sentries to alert her if something went amiss and descended from the battlements to join the cavalry formation.

She didn't get far.

The sentry's report confirmed what her ears told her: fighting had erupted outside the fort's walls. No one knew who had started it, but that mattered not. She vaulted atop her mount, drew her sword, ordered the gates open, and led the finest horse-warriors of Brydein to the High King's defense.

Gwenhwyfach lost herself in a swirl of sight and sound and stench as battle frenzy overcame her. Imagining that Gyan was fighting at her side, she hacked and slashed toward Arthur's last known position, her sword falling with lethal precision. When she was pulled from her horse, she scrambled to her feet, fought off her attackers, and battled the rest of the way on foot.

No one who crossed swords with Gwenhwyfach ferch Arthur survived unscathed. Countless warriors didn't survive at all.

# TWINS

Her opponents dwindled as the afternoon waned, the clash of arms replaced by the screams of the wounded and dying. During a lull, Gwenhwyfach glanced around. Some men were fleeing into the distance; whose, she couldn't tell. Others were feebly moving in the fading light. Most lay still. The Atan ran red.

Weary beyond measure, Gwenhwyfach began the search for her father, not calling his name lest his men fear the worst and lose heart. Not far from the oak she found Medraut, a bloody hole in his chest and his eyes staring into eternity. Despite the way he had treated her at the end, she couldn't blame him for feeling betrayed by the choices she and Yfarryn had made. She sank to her knees beside his body, head bowed, regret flooding her soul.

A hand on her shoulder made her start. She looked up, astonished to see the tear-streaked face of Morghe bending over her, an ocean of anguish threatening to burst through the trembling of her chin. Her own emotions and fatigue prevented her from questioning her aunt's presence.

"I—" Gwenhwyfach sighed, daubing her eyes with the least bloody portion of her glove. "I really did love him. I wish I could have made him see that."

Arthur's sister drew a deep breath and held it. After a moment, her face molded into an expression of resolve. "Medraut wasn't the only one who failed to see love where it was offered freely and without reservation."

Gwenhwyfach felt her eyebrows lower. She wanted to ask Morghe what she'd meant when she saw a dour-faced Bedwyr approaching them.

"Quickly, Lady Gwenhwyfach, Lady Morghe. He needs our help."

Harboring no doubt which "he" Bedwyr was talking about, Gwenhwyfach rose. She and Morghe followed him to where Arthur lay propped against the oak's trunk. His eyes were closed, his face pinched and gray. He was breathing in shallow, ragged gasps. His head and abdomen were bleeding profusely.

Morghe tore strips from her underdress and pressed them to the wounds. Her anguished plea for forgiveness dissolved into weeping.

Arthur opened his eyes, and his lips bent into a faint smile. Morghe's cries calmed. She nodded, rose, and reached for the wine skin, cup, and pouch she had brought. After pouring a measure, she asked Bedwyr to hold the cup while she added herbs from her pouch.

Gwenhwyfach shook her head with incredulity. How a lifetime of rancor and malice could be overcome in the space of a hundred heartbeats lay far beyond her ken. But she cared less for her aunt's apparent change of heart than for the figure she was tending. She moved to Arthur's other side and knelt to grasp his hand.

His grip tightened, and he gazed at her. "Gwenhwyfach. Thank God. You hurt?"

Cut, bruised, and aching in muscles forgotten during her imprisonment—she shook her head.

Morghe stooped and tried to hold the cup to his lips, but he jerked his head aside.

"Drink, you old fool," Morghe insisted. "For the pain."

He grimaced. "Indeed. No pain on the far side of death." But he drank the concoction. The tension in his face lessened.

"Dear brother, you wound me," Morghe said. "I'm trying to help you."

"You've never done anything that hasn't suited your own ends. However altruistic they might appear."

"True enough. But not this day."

Arthur lowered his eyebrows. "How did you know...?"

Morghe barked a grim laugh. "I am Morriga incarnate. I scented battle, assumed raven form, and flew here."

"To pick my bones clean and call yourself High Queen."

"No." She bowed her head. When she raised it again, her cheeks glistened with tears. "Please believe me, Arthur. I am truly sorry. For—for everything." She swiped at her eyes and reached out with a fresh cloth to daub Arthur's head wound.

"My quest for power is done. It died"—she nodded toward Medraut's corpse—"there."

Arthur held Morghe's gaze for a long time. Whatever silent communication passed between them, Gwenhwyfach had no clue. He nodded once and regarded Bedwyr. "Report."

"Cai, Gawain, Gareth, Angusel, Uwain, Culhwch, Peredur, Bohort, all dead, and most of their men with them. An even higher casualty rate for Medraut's side." No triumph gilded Bedwyr's tone. "The ravens have won this day, Arthur."

"Ravens don't concern me." Arthur released Gwenhwyfach's hand to gesture at his sword. "Take it, Bedwyr, and throw it into the firth."

"But why, Father? Surely the next High King—"

"Won't want a weapon stained with the blood of his people." He drew a shuddering breath. "If there is a next High King." Wincing, Arthur turned his gaze upon Bedwyr. "You have your orders, old friend." Trying to hide the quiver of his chin with a sharp nod, Bedwyr grasped the sheathed sword and thrust it into his belt. To Morghe, Arthur said, "Gwenhwyfar?"

"I shall bring her here." Morghe rose, mounted her mare, wheeled the animal toward Caer Lugubalion, and set off.

Gwenhwyfach glanced at her father. He had closed his eyes, the pinched look returning to his face. Her heart lurched. Giving him another swallow of Morghe's wine, she prayed Yfarryn would make it in time.

---

YFARRYN WAS sitting alone in her chambers, wondering what in heaven's name was happening, when she heard someone converse with the guard outside her door. The female voice with an unmistakable air of authority could mean only one person.

"Morghe!" she said when the door swung open, confirming her guess. Gone was all trace of arrogant posturing. In fact, her aunt looked downright worried. "What's wrong?"

"Ready yourself. Your father is dying."

Surprise propelled Yfarryn to her feet. "What? No! It can't be—you're lying!"

"Am I?" Morghe planted hands on hips. "Meet me in the stables and come see for yourself." She turned with a flourish of her black cloak and strode from the chamber.

Despite the awkwardness inflicted upon her by Lannchu's child, Yfarryn had never moved so fast in her life.

As a stable hand saddled and bridled Yfarryn's mare, Morghe described what she knew of the battle, Medraut's death, and the deaths of other men Yfarryn had admired all her life. What Morghe couldn't explain, the corpse-strewn Camboglanna battlefield supplied in gut-wrenching detail.

Letting her horse pick its way through the ruined siege camp, Morghe led Yfarryn toward a lone oak, where she saw two figures crouched beside a third. One soldier stood. Bedwyr, she realized. He saluted and strode toward the river, her father's sword in his fist. Puzzled, Yfarryn halted her mare to watch him, as did Morghe. Where the waters ran deepest, he stopped, faced Arthur, and offered a final salute with Caleberyllus before turning to fling it away. Tumbling hilt over point, it flashed golden in the sunset's last rays and disappeared into the river.

"Why?" Yfarryn cried, hoarse with anguish.

Morghe's look was not unsympathetic. "He commanded it." She nudged her mount forward.

Feeling numb, Yfarryn followed. Her next surprise came with the realization that the other person attending her father was her sister. Fach looked relieved as she held the reins for Yfarryn to dismount. On impulse, in spite of Fach's grimy and blood-smeared armor, Yfarryn embraced her. The only words she could trust herself to whisper were, "I'm so sorry."

"As am I—more than you can know." Fach nodded toward their father, who was watching them through pain-hazed eyes. "But you must tell him that."

Fighting her tears, Yfarryn rushed to his side. As she knelt and took his hand in both of hers, the sobs won.

"I'm past the need for tears, my child." Though weak, the affection in his tone was clear. "Cry for Brydein."

"You are Brydein, Father. And always will be." That coaxed a wan smile from him, and another sob threatened to choke off what Yfarryn needed to say. She swallowed it. "I—my selfishness brought you to this. Can—can you forgive me?"

He made a brief circling motion with his hand. "We all had a part in it. I forgive you for yours." His palm felt cold against her cheek. "You must forgive yourself." His eyes unfocused, and Yfarryn wondered what he was seeing. A ghost of a smile touched his lips. "Gyan is impatient..." He looked at Yfarryn, gaze lucid. "Please forgive me, daughter," he whispered, "for not letting you follow your heart."

"But I did." She pressed his hand to her belly. The child kicked, and she hoped he felt it too. "Here is the future of Brydein, Father."

His smile deepened, and he beckoned Fach closer. She knelt on his other side. "I trust you both to guard it well." His eyes drifted shut and did not open again.

Guarding the future, Yfarryn realized as her tears flowed unchecked, was the only honorable task left.

# Chapter 5
## The Aftermath

At Arbroch, stronghold of Gyan's people, a year and a half after Arthur's death, Gwenhwyfach ferch Arthur watched her nephew totter about the main yard, clinging to his mother's skirts and getting his introduction to snow. She tried to forget that it was the second anniversary of her ill-fated wedding to Medraut and that he had not left his legacy with her as Lannchu had done with her sister. Regret could be an insidious stealer of hope if given half a chance.

Meirbi let go, determined to explore this frosty new world on his own. He slipped and fell, bumping his forehead on the frozen ground. Yfarryn scooped her crying son into her arms, stroking his head and murmuring soothing words.

One day, the twins would teach Meirbi that his name was based upon the Caledonian phrase *meur a'beir*, "branch of the bear," an homage to the Brytoni portion of his exalted heritage. And they would have to humble themselves to explain why his name was not Meirbi mac Gwenhwyfar, in the Caledonian tradition, or even Meirbi mac Lannchu, but Meirbi mac Artyr.

There would be time aplenty for those lessons later. Now was the season to dry tears, to heal, and to nurture hope.

# About the Story

WHEN ONE HAS certain life commitments and responsibilities, it takes a long time to put words to paper, to say nothing of the time it takes to whip those words into publishable shape and deliver the product into the public's hands. I have been working on my 8-book series, The Dragon's Dove Chronicles, for more than a quarter of a century, and each of the eight installments exists in some stage of completion.

"Twins" represents the most unique stage, being excerpted from Book 6 of The Dragon's Dove Chronicles, *Sundown of a Dream*. The short story began life in early 2000, soon after I had learned of an Arthurian anthology that was accepting submissions. The anthology passed on my submission in favor of a work of roughly the same length that rehashed Sir Thomas Malory's *Le Morte d'Arthur* without contributing any new insights to the major characters.

Thus "Twins" languished until 2017 when, encouraged by students in a college Arthurian literature class to whom I had delivered a lecture, I decided to offer it to my growing fan base while I finished *Raging Sea*. Since my writing is much angstier these days, *Sundown of a Dream* will most likely bear little resemblance to "Twins," but I hope you enjoy it nonetheless and will encourage your fellow readers to pick up this and other of my works.

# About the Art

YFARRYN IS REPRESENTED by the Elgin Beast, a carving on a Pictish standing stone found in Elgin, Moray, Scotland. The "Pictish beast"—so named because nobody quite knows whether the creature is intended to represent an elephant, a dolphin, or some animal that's now extinct—is quite common in ancient Pictish stone art, but the Elgin Beast with its elaborate Celtic interlacing is one of the fancier examples of the form. I selected it for Yfarryn's glyph because to me it symbolizes her fusion as a child of Caledonach (Pictish) and Brytoni (Celtic) cultures.

The "Z-rod" of the militant Gwenhwyfach's glyph is a detail on the front of the Dyce 1 stone, located in the city of Aberdeen, Scotland. The Z-rod—with the *z* sometimes facing forward and sometimes backward, as in the Dyce 1 example—is another iconic Pictish symbol embellished in unique and fanciful ways. The *z* reminds me of a spear that is perhaps decorated with feathers or barbs, and the wide rod terminating in discs represents either a style of cloak fastening or a sword belt. Gwenhwyfach, of course, would insist upon the latter interpretation.

The following twin kelpies, planned for the cover of *Sundown of a Dream*, are found on the same side as the cross on stone Aberlemno 2, on display under cover in Aberlemno Kirkyard, Forfar, Angus, Scotland. The kelpie is not as common a symbol in Pictish art as the other two are, and this carving is one of the most impressive I've seen either in person or in photographs. These creatures represent the fact that the lives of Gyan's twin daughters—and the lives of those they love—are inseparably intertwined for all time.

# People

ENTRY FORMAT:
**FULL NAME (Pronunciation).** Brief description, which may include rank, occupation, clan, country, nickname(s), name's origin and meaning, banner, and legendary name. Place-names are given in the person's native language. Pronunciations are approximate; when in doubt, pronounce it however it makes sense to you! Many of the names also may be heard in the audiobook edition of *Dawnflight*.

**ALAYNA (AH-LAH-EE-NAH).** Late Chieftainess and Àrd-Banoigin of Clan Alban, Caledon. Angusel's mother. Name origin: Scottish Gaelic *àlainn* ("beautiful, elegant, splendid").

**ANGUSEL MAC Alayna.** Chieftain of Clan Alban, Caledon. Son of Alayna and Guilbach. Name origin: inspired by Scottish Gaelic *an càs* ("the trying situation"), *sàl* ("sea"). Legendary name: Sir Lancelot du Lac.

**ANNAMAR FERCH Gorlas.** Daughter of Gorlas and Ygraine; Arthur's half sister; wife of Loth; mother of Gawain, Gareth, and Medraut. Clan: Cwrnwyll, Rheged, Brydein. Legendary name: Queen Margause.

**ARTHUR MAP Uther.** High King of Brydein. Son of Uther and Ygraine; brother of Morghe; husband of Gyanhumara; father of Gwenhwyfar and Gwenhwyfach. Clan: Cwrnwyll, Brydein.

Nickname: Artyr. Banner: scarlet dragon rampant on gold. Legendary name: King Arthur Pendragon.

**BEDWYR (BAYD-VEER).** Highest-ranking officer of the Brytoni fleet. Clan: Lammor, Gododdin, Brydein. Legendary name: Sir Bedivere.

**BOHORT.** CENTURION in the Dragon Legion of the Brytoni army. Legendary name: Sir Bors de Ganis.

**CAI.** LEGATE of the Dragon Legion of the Brytoni army. Arthur's foster brother. Legendary name: Sir Kay the Seneschal.

**CULHWCH (KEEL-HOOK).** One of the cohort commanders of the Lion Legion of the Brytoni army.

**DAFYDD (DAH-VEETH).** Abbot of St. Padraic's Monastery. Name origin: Brythonic variant of the name David.

**EILEANN (EE-LAY-AHN).** Wife of Angusel; mother of Lannchu. Clan: Tarsuinn, Caledon. Name origin: Scottish Gaelic *eileann* ("island"). Legendary name: Lady Elaine.

**GARETH MAP Loth.** Chieftain of Clan Lothian. Second son of Loth and Annamar; Arthur's nephew. Banner: amber bear on forest green. Legendary name: Sir Gareth.

**GAWAIN MAP Loth.** Legate of the Lion Legion of the Brytoni army. Firstborn son of Loth and Annamar; Arthur's nephew. Legendary name: Sir Gawain.

**GORLAS.** LATE Chieftain of Clan Cwrnwyll of Rheged, Brydein. Ygraine's first husband; father of Annamar. Legendary name: Duke Gorlois of Cornwall.

# TWINS

**GUILBACH (GOOL-BAHK).** Late Chieftain of Clan Alban, Caledon. Alayna's consort; Angusel's father. Clan: Tarsuinn, Caledon. Name origin: Scottish Gaelic *guilbneach* ("curlew").

**GWENHWYFACH (GWEN-IH-VAHK) ferch Arthur.** Second daughter of Gyanhumara and Arthur; twin sister of Gwenhwyfar nic Gyanhumara. Nickname: Fach (VAHK). Name origin: This is the name of the "false Guinevere" mentioned in an Old Welsh triad. Nickname origin: Welsh *fach* ("small").

**GWENHWYFAR (GWEN-IH-VAR) nic Gyanhumara.** Firstborn daughter of Gyanhumara and Arthur; twin sister of Gwenhwyfach ferch Arthur. Nickname: Yfarryn (ee-VAHR-een). Name origin: Brythonic *gwenhwyfar* ("white shadow"). Nickname origin: Welsh *y farryn* ("the bar").

**GYANHUMARA (GHEE-AHN-HUH-MAR-AH) nic Hymar.** Late Chieftainess of Clan Argyll of Caledon, and High Queen of Brydein. Daughter of Hymar; half sister of Peredur; wife of Arthur; mother of Gwenhwyfar and Gwenhwyfach. Nickname: Gyan (GHEE-ahn). Banner: two silver doves flying, on dark blue. Name origin: Scottish Gaelic *gainne amhran* ("rarest song"). Legendary names: Queen Guinevere, Guenevere, Guenever.

**HYMAR (HEE-MAR).** Late Chieftainess and Àrd-Banoigin of Clan Argyll, Caledon. Mother of Peredur and Gyanhumara. Name origin: Scottish Gaelic *amhran* ("song").

**LANNCHU (LAN-COO) mac Eileann.** Son of Eileann and Angusel; a centurion in the Lion Legion of the Brytoni army. Name origin: Scottish Gaelic *lann chu* ("hound's blade").

**LOTH (LOTE).** Late Chieftain of Clan Lothian of Gododdin, Brydein. Annamar's husband; father of Gawain, Gareth, and Medraut. Legendary name: King Lot.

**Lucius.** Fictional non-Roman emperor of Rome.

**Medraut map Loth.** Third son of Loth and Annamar; Arthur's nephew. Clan: Lothian, Gododdin, Brydein. Legendary names: Sir Mordred, Modred.

**Meirbi mac Artyr.** Son of Gwenhwyfar and Lannchu; named in honor of his maternal grandfather, Arthur. Name origin: inspired by Scottish Gaelic *meur a'beir* ("branch of the bear").

**Morghe (MOR-gheh) ferch Uther.** Daughter of Uther and Ygraine; Arthur's younger sister. Legendary name: Queen Morgan Le Fay.

**Peredur (PARE-eh-dur) mac Hymar.** Prefect of the Horse Cohort of the Brytoni army. Hymar's son; Gyanhumara's half brother. Clan: Argyll, Caledon. Name origin: Scottish Gaelic *pòr dùr* ("stubborn seed"). Legendary name: Sir Percival.

**Urien (OO-ree-ehn).** Late Chieftain of Clan Moray, Dalriada, Brydein. Husband of Morghe; father of Uwain. Legendary names: King Urien, Uriens.

**Uther.** Late commander-in-chief of the Brytoni army. Ygraine's second husband; father of Arthur and Morghe.

**Uwain (OO-vane) map Urien.** Officer in the Brytoni army. Son of Urien and Morghe; Arthur's nephew.

**Ygraine (EE-GRAY-neh).** Late Chieftainess of Clan Cwrnwyll of Rheged, Brydein. Mother (with Gorlas) of Annamar, mother (with Uther) of Arthur and Morghe. Legendary name: Queen Igraine.

# Glossary

THIS APPENDIX INCLUDES place-names and foreign terms. Pronunciation guidelines are supplied for the less obvious terms, especially those of Brythonic or Scottish Gaelic origin. In the case of a term having multiple translations used in the text, the most commonly referenced term is listed first. Word and phrase origins are given wherever possible.

My choices of word selection, translation, spelling, suggested pronunciation, and the use of accent marks reflect an attempt to imply a "proto-language" to today's version, especially with regard to the Scottish-Gaelic-based words, compounds, and phrases. Terms identified as having a Pictish source are based on studies of Scottish place-names, since there are no known documents that were written in ancient Pictish. Brythonic-sourced words are derived from ancient Welsh literature, such as the *Mabinogion*.

**ALBAN ("THE Wild People"), Clan.** Caledonaiche: *Albainaich Chaledon*. The clan's name tracks to the ancient name for Scotland and is deliberately evocative of an alternate legendary name for Arthur's realm, "Albion." Banner: rampant white lion on cerulean blue. Cloak pattern: sky blue crossed with crimson and green. Gemstone: aquamarine. Name origin: inspired by Scottish Gaelic *am bàn* ("untilled") and *Albainn* ("Alba," "Scotland").

**Antonine Wall, the.** Latin: *Antoninorum murum*. Frontier fortification built in southern Scotland by Roman Emperor Antoninus Pius in the mid-second century A.D. Extends from the Firth of Forth to the Firth of Clyde.

**Arbroch (Caledonaiche, "Exalted Town").** Brytonic: *Ardoca*. Latin: *Alauna Veniconum*. Seat of Clan Argyll and home fortress of Gyanhumara; Roman fort captured in the first century A.D. by the Caledonaich, located near the present-day village of Braco in Perthshire, Scotland. Caledonaiche origin: Scottish Gaelic *àrd* ("exalted"), *broch* ("burgh").

**Àrd-banoigin (aird-ban-UH-ghin; pl. àrd-banoigainn; Caledonaiche, "exalted heir-bearer(s)").** The female member of the ruling family through whom the clan's line of succession is determined. Typically, the clan's chieftainess serves as àrd-banoigin while she is of childbearing age and passes this status to a daughter or niece when the younger woman reaches physical maturity. Origin: Scottish Gaelic *àrd* ("exalted"), *ban* ("woman"), *oighre* ("heir"), *gin* ("beget").

**Argyll (AR-gayeel; "The Tempestuous People"), Clan.** Caledonaiche: *Argaillanaich Chaledon*. The clan's name tracks to the former County of Argyll, Scotland. Banner: two silver mourning doves in flight, on dark blue. Cloak pattern: dark blue crossed with saffron and scarlet. Gemstone: sapphire. Name origin: Scottish Gaelic *ar gailleann* ("our tempest").

**Atan.** Caledonaiche: *Ab Atan* ("The Swelling River"). Latin: *Itouna*. Brytonic: *Ituna*. The Eden River of the Eden District of Cumbria, England, a tributary of the Solway Firth. Name origins: Scottish Gaelic *at* ("to swell"), Brythonic *ituna* ("rushing"). The Latin version is a variant of the Brythonic word.

**Brydein (Brytonic).** Latin: *Britannia*. Britain.

**Brytoni.** Of or pertaining to the inhabitants of western and mid-Brydein.

**Brytonic.** The native language of the Brytons, also known as "Brythonic" or *P-Celtic* in present-day anthropological usage.

**Caer Lugubalion (Brytonic, "Fort of Lugh's Strength").** Latin: *Luguvalium* ("Lugh's Valley"). Brytoni-controlled fortress near the western end of Hadrian's Wall, headquarters of the Dragon Legion of Brydein, located in what is now Carlisle, Cumbria, England.

**Caleberyllus (Latin, "Burning Jewel").** Arthur's sword, known through various sources as Caliburnus, Caliburn, Caledfwlch, and Excalibur. This name is my invention, derived from the Latin words *calere* (heat, origin of "calorie") and *beryllus* (beryl, a classification of gem) as a poetic description of the sword's distinguishing feature. Technically, a ruby is a cabochon, not a beryl, but I suspect that nobody was making that fine a distinction in the fifth century A.D.

**Caledon (poss. Chaledon; Caledonaiche, "(of the) Place of the Hard People").** The name the Caledonaich apply to their territory, encompassing what is now the Scottish Highlands and northern Lowlands. Origin: Pictish/proto-Celtic *caled* ("hard").

**Caledonach ("Caledonian"), Caledonaich ("Caledonians" and "The Hard People"), Caledonaiche ("Caledonian language"), Chaledonach ("Caledonian's" or "of the Caledonian"), Chaledonaich ("Caledonians'" or "of the Caledonians").** Idiomatic terms of my own invention, based on Scottish Gaelic linguistic rules for indicating group membership (*-ach* (sing.) and *-aich* (pl.) suffixes), and the possessive form (*Ch-* prefix). Language designation (*-aiche* suffix) is my own invention.

**Caledonia (Latin).** The name that Latin- and Brytonic-speakers apply to the home of the Caledonaich, the region encompassing what is now the Scottish Highlands and northern Lowlands.

**Caledonian(s).** Of or pertaining to the inhabitants of the nation of Caledonia, terms used by Latin- and Brytonic-speakers.

**Calends.** The first day of any month on the Roman calendar—and the origin of the word "calendar." Origin: Latin *kalendae* ("the called").

**Camboglanna (Brytonic, "Crooked Bank").** Fortress near the western end of Hadrian's wall, built on a high bluff overlooking the Cambog (Cambeck) Valley, located in present-day Castlesteads, Cumbria, England.

**Clan-mark.** A tattoo representing the Caledonach clan's symbol, usually painted with woad dye. A woman receives the clan-mark on her right forearm when she achieves the status of àrd-banoigin.

**Cwrnwyll (keern-weedl), Clan.** Brytoni clan occupying the region of Rheged. I invented this clan name to be evocative of Cornwall, the region ascribed by tradition for Arthur's birth. Banner: rampant ivory unicorn on crimson. Cloak pattern: dark red crossed with sky-blue and saffron. Gemstone: ruby.

**Dalriada (Latin).** Political region in the northwest sector of Brydein consisting chiefly of the Kintyre Peninsula and western islands of Scotland.

**Dragon Legion, the.** Latin: *Legio Draconis*. Northern Brytoni army unit, whence the term "Pendragon" originates.

**Dun Eidyn (Brytonic, "Fort of Eidyn").** Home fortress of Medraut, a hill-fort on the summit of what is known today as Arthur's Seat, Edinburgh, Scotland, located on the south bank of the Firth of Forth.

**Ferch (VERK, Brytonic).** "Daughter of," followed by the father's name; e.g., Morghe ferch Uther.

**Gododdin (go-DOTH-in).** Brytoni-controlled territory corresponding to modern southeastern Scotland and northeastern England. The name is derived from the Latin name of the Celtic tribe inhabiting the area at the time of the Roman occupation, the Votadini.

**Hadrian's Wall.** Latin: *Hadriani murum*. Frontier fortification built in northern Britain by the Roman Emperor Hadrian early in the second century A.D. Extends from Wallsend on the River Tyne through Carlisle to the Solway Firth near Bowness-on-Solway.

**Lammor, Clan (Brytonic).** Brytoni clan of the region of Strathclyd, Brydein. Banner: emerald-green stag's head on silver. Cloak pattern: grass-green crossed with silver and black. Gemstone: heliodor. Name origin: inspired by the Lammermuir Hills of southern Scotland, where this clan is located.

**Lion Legion, the.** Latin: *Legio Leonis*. Northern Brytoni army unit.

**Lothian, Clan (Brytonic).** Brytoni clan of the region of Gododdin, Brydein. Banner: rearing amber bear on dark green. Cloak pattern: forest green crossed with dark blue and gold. Gemstone: amber.

**Lugh.** Caledonach/Brytoni Lord of Light, symbolized by a bull.

**Mac (Caledonaiche).** "Son of," followed by the mother's name; e.g., Angusel mac Alayna. Origin: Scottish Gaelic.

**Map (Northern Brytonic).** "Son of," followed by the father's name; e.g., Arthur map Uther. Brytons of southern clans use the variant *ap*, also in conjunction with the father's name.

**Maun.** Latin: *Mavnum*. Isle of Man in the Irish Sea.

**Mo ghaolag (mo HAY-lahg, Caledonaiche, "my little love").** A term of endearment. Origin: Scottish Gaelic (colloquially, "my sweetheart").

**Mo leannan (Caledonaiche, "my beloved spouse").** A unisex term of endearment used between married couples. Origin: Scottish Gaelic.

**Moray, Clan.** Brytoni clan occupying the region of Dalriada, Brydein. Banner: black boar on gold. Cloak pattern: black crossed with gold. Gemstone: jet.

**Morriga.** Caledonian/Brytoni deity symbolized by a comb and mirror. Often associated with war, death, and fertility.

**Na Lann-Seolta (Caledonaiche, "of the Blade-Cunning").** The title bestowed upon Angusel for becoming the best swordsman in the world. Origin: Scottish Gaelic *na* ("of the") *lann* ("blade"), *seòlta* ("cunning", "skillful").

**Nemetona.** Caledonach/Brytoni Goddess of War, symbolized by a lioness, said to drive a crimson chariot drawn by four winged, fire-snorting black mares.

**Nic (Caledonaiche).** "Daughter of," followed by the mother's name; e.g., Gyanhumara nic Hymar. Origin: Scottish Gaelic, contraction of *nighean mhic* ("young woman offspring").

**PENDRAGON, THE.** Brytonic: *Y Ddraig Pen* ("The Chief Dragon"). Latin: *Draconis Rex* ("Dragon King"). Caledonaiche: *Àrd-Ceann Teine-Beathach Mór* ("High-Chief Great Fire-Beast"). Honorific applied to the commander-in-chief of the Brytoni army.

**PORT DHOO-GLASS (Manx).** Brytoni-controlled port named for its location at the confluence of the rivers Dhoo ("Black") and Glass ("Green"), present-day Douglas, Isle of Man.

**PRAETORIUM (LATIN, "governor's residence").** The living quarters of the garrison commander; also may be translated as "palace."

**RHEGED (BRYTONIC).** Political region of Brydein encompassing what is now northern England and southern Scotland.

**SAINT PADRAIC'S Isle.** Islet off the western coast of Maun; site of Saint Padraic's Monastery. Present-day St. Patrick's Isle.

**SAINT PADRAIC'S Monastery.** Christian men's religious community founded by St. Padraic (Patrick) in the mid-5th century, located on Saint Padraic's Isle and presided over by an abbot. Site corresponds to Peel Castle, St. Patrick's Isle, which existed as a Celtic monastery for several centuries, until the Vikings turned it into a fortification.

**SCARLET DRAGON, the.** Standard of the Brytoni army, a scarlet dragon pacing on a field of gold, very similar to the present flag of Wales.

**SENAUDON (CALEDONAICHE, "Place of Charmed Protection").** Angusel's home fortress located in present-day Stirling, Scotland. Origin: inspired by Scottish Gaelic *seun* ("a charm for protection" and "to defend by charms").

**Tarsuinn ("The Crossing People"), Clan.** Caledonaiche: *Tarsuinnaich Chaledon*. Caledonach clan that runs a large ferry business from several points across the Firth of Forth. Banner: gold falcon in flight, on azure. Cloak pattern: saffron crossed with blue and red. Gemstone: golden beryl. Name origin: Scottish Gaelic *tarsainn* ("across").

**Tòn (Caledonaiche).** A euphemism for a male body part. Origin: Scottish Gaelic *tòn* ("the fundament").

# About the Author

Photo Copyright © by Chris Headlee

KIM HEADLEE LIVES on a farm in the mountains of southwestern Virginia with her family, cats, goats, Great Pyrenees goat guards, and assorted wildlife. People and creatures come and go, but the cave and the 250-year-old house ruins—the latter having been occupied as recently as the midtwentieth century—seem to be sticking around for a while yet.

http://www.kimheadlee.com
https://twitter.com/KimHeadlee
http://www.facebook.com/kimiversonheadlee

## Other published works by Kim Iverson Headlee:

*The Business of Writing*, nonfiction e-book and paperback, Pendragon Cove Press, 2017.

*Raging Sea: Enemies and Allies*, part 2 of The Dragon's Dove Chronicles, book 3, e-book, Pendragon Cove Press, 2016.

"Kings", a sword & sorcery crossover novella by Kim Iverson Headlee and Patricia Duffy Novak, e-book, audiobook, and paperback, Pendragon Cove Press, 2016.

*King Arthur's Sister in Washington's Court* by Mark Twain as channeled by Kim Iverson Headlee, illustrated by Jennifer Doneske and Tom Doneske, hardcover, paperback, audiobook, and e-book, Lucky Bat Books, 2015.

*Raging Sea: Reckonings*, part 1 of The Dragon's Dove Chronicles, book 3, e-book, Pendragon Cove Press, 2015.

"The Challenge," a Dragon's Dove Chronicles novella, e-book, audiobook, and paperback, Pendragon Cove Press, 2015.

*Liberty*, second edition, with character-totem art by Jessica Headlee, e-book and paperback, Pendragon Cove Press, 2014.

*Snow in July*, with character-totem art by Jessica Headlee, e-book & paperback, Pendragon Cove Press, 2014.

"The Color of Vengeance," a short story excerpted from *Morning's Journey*, e-book & audiobook, Lucky Bat Books, 2013; paperback, Pendragon Cove Press, 2015.

*Morning's Journey*, The Dragon's Dove Chronicles, book 2, e-book and paperback, Lucky Bat Books, 2013; cover and interior updated 2014.

*Dawnflight*, second edition, The Dragon's Dove Chronicles, book 1, e-book, audiobook, and paperback, Lucky Bat Books, 2013; cover and interior updated 2014.

*Liberty* by Kimberly Iverson, first edition, paperback, HQN Books, Harlequin, 2006.

*Dawnflight* by Kim Headlee, first edition, paperback, Sonnet Books, Simon & Schuster, 1999.

## Forthcoming:

*Raging Sea: Crucible of Combat*, part 3 of The Dragon's Dove Chronicles, book 3, Pendragon Cove Press.

*Prophecy*, the sequel to *Liberty*, Pendragon Cove Press.

*Dawnflight*
Amazon ebook

Amazon
paperback

Audiobook

*Morning's Journey* Amazon ebook

Amazon
paperback

Made in the USA
Columbia, SC
01 May 2018